Making Our Mark

Student stories and creative conversations about the world of work

Curated by
DAWN REEVES
on behalf of
PROFESSOR JUDITH BURNETT
UNIVERSITY OF GREENWICH
STUDENT EXPERIENCE PROJECT

First paperback edition published in Great Britain in 2015 by Shared Press

Published by Shared Press
www.sharedpress.co.uk

Copyright © Dawn Reeves 2015

The right of Dawn Reeves has been asserted by her in accordance with the Copyright, Designs and Patents Act 1988.

A catalogue record for this book is available from the British Library.

ISBN 978-0-9574981-5-0

All rights reserved. No part of this publication may be reproduced, transmitted, or stored in a retrieval system, in any form or by any means without the prior written permission of the publisher.

All characters in the flash fiction in this publication are fictitious and any resemblance to real persons, living or dead, is purely coincidental.

Designed and typeset by Quarto Design
www.quartodesign.com

Edited by Lisa Hughes
www.completefiction.co.uk

Shared Press' policy is to use papers that are natural, renewable and recyclable products from well managed forests in accordance with the rules of the Forest Stewardship Council.

"Making your mark on the world is hard. If it were easy, everybody would do it. But it's not. It takes patience, it takes commitment, and it comes with plenty of failure along the way. The real test is not whether you avoid this failure, because you won't. It's whether you let it harden or shame you into inaction, or whether you learn from it; whether you choose to persevere."

— Barack Obama

Contents

Foreword

This summer our university's 'class of 2015' will embark on life after university. If they choose to remain in London and the South East of England, they will join graduates from all over the UK who will move to this region over the next two years. If they choose to relocate or travel, they will join others who also choose to do so. They will meet, conflict and create with their cohort, its neighbours and the large world beyond. They will compete for jobs, housing and status. They will embark on personal projects of many different kinds in their drive to find a place in a world where the question of their identity can no longer be answered by the words 'I am a student' and work – whatever that is and however that is conducted – will become part of the answer.

There is a rising tide of social anxiety about employment prospects for graduates. The introduction of student loans and the 'realisation' that massive sums of loan money will, quite possibly, never be repaid has upped the ante somewhat. Like never before the value of a university education is being questioned: business, government, the general public and wider society, as well as the student body, their parents, tutors and employers, are prone to ask about the fate of the graduate. What does come next? What difference did university really make? How are they making their mark?

Many of our students are very successful at making their mark, but there are challenges and, surprisingly, we know relatively little about students' expectations and experiences of work, however it is defined: paid, unpaid, employed, self-employed, contracted, volunteered, recognised, enterprised. This is particularly so when it comes to understanding what the *vision* for an active working life might be.

In most universities nowadays large numbers of students work, many will arrive at the doors of the university already one career down, sometimes well advanced with a few different jobs or roles in tow. Less experienced students will still have undertaken economic activity of some kind, and may expect and actively look for work throughout their studies. Universities, along with many other kinds of organisations, provide services to support successful engagement with work, both at a higher order of inventory, desire, skill and experience, as well as at a more tactical level, such as interview techniques or how to construct a CV. What we know less about is how students see it, what they feel about it and, for them, what does 'work' mean.

Making Our Mark arose out of the bones of another project, Follow That Student, in which I trailed a cohort of students for a university year, kindly aided by the student intern, Nusrath Ahmed. One of the things which emerged was how difficult it was to find time to meet to chat – because so many of the students were working or doing 'activities' of various kinds as well as studying! Nonetheless, on graduation, it seemed that many weren't able to slide effortlessly into work, change the job they already had, or upgrade the job they already did to a graduate job. Instead, they remained in largely local labour markets, often in part-time and poorly remunerated roles. I began to see both the struggle of the transition and the different experiences of managing uncertainty and developing resilience, although there was some interesting behaviour, including acts of ingenuity and sheer bullishness, and far more students are attempting self-employment and portfolio livelihoods than might popularly be imagined.

There are many explanations for what happens in 'life after university', but an insight into visions of work may be valuable to both students and the university, which accepts it has a role in supporting students to get from A to B: one starting point is to know the A from which we begin and the nature of the B to which we might be travelling.

Given the fog factor in articulating a vision for work, we offered creative writing and received back creativity in many forms. The pieces in this book are from students who responded to an advert or a nudge from a friendly tutor, and they represent an album of ideas, visions, biographies and visuals around the theme of work. The boundaries are blurred for many and there is a reality in these pages that work is not filed tidily into a box marked 'work', but the contributions form a rich and stimulating riff on work.

This project was led by Dawn Reeves, a brilliant facilitator with years of experience and insight into all things economic and creative – Dawn is someone who really can walk into a room of students and walk out with a book. She was assisted by our student intern, Abas Abow, and my PA, Sheila, as well as faculty staff who kindly encouraged students to take part. Of course, Making Our Mark could not have happened without the enthusiasm and input of our fantastic students.

Professor Judith Burnett FHEA, FRSA, ACIM
Pro Vice-Chancellor Architecture, Computing, Humanities
May 2015

Introduction

Stories and conversations

Work is at the heart of what we do, how we live and who we are. The world of work is a place where we play out the stories of our lives; where we travel through strange lands, experience trials and face adversity; where we learn and grow, realise our hopes and dreams. This book is a vibrant, creative take on the world of work from the perspective of students who are thinking about their futures.

In the stories, conversations and indeed images in this book, we see the world through the eyes of students passing through the University of Greenwich. While the harsh economics are that many of them need to work to pay their way, most are nonetheless feeling their way, imagining possibilities, and they don't yet know how they will reach their potential and feel fulfilled.

There are no stereotypes in this book. You'll encounter very different people, experiences and expectations; you'll find incredible diversity. These students are jugglers, grafters and explorers, and although they exhibit aspiration and uncertainty, they are alive with imagination, energy and talent.

There are tales from first years who have recently left school and one who has a successful career of 30 years behind her. There are second-year students already working part-time in a managerial capacity, third years who have been involved with start-up ventures, and a fourth year who has registered two patents for a large international company.

Encouraging contributions

To discover these stories we took a deliberately inclusive approach, sent out mass email invites, asked around for volunteers and turned up at the end of lectures to spread the word. We asked students to write fiction, to tell tales and visually illustrate their stories about work, and we gave them choice, flexibility and support to share their views in different formats.

We facilitated two creative thinking and writing workshops, which included an invitation to students to contribute to the book in the form of flash fiction. This is a brief form of literature that challenges writers to tell their tale in a few hundred words. It's liberating, but safe, and at around a page in length, it's very doable and accessible for people who haven't written creatively before.

We also invited students to take part in creative conversations, which enabled us to collaborate on the individual pen pictures of students, and contribute pieces of work that they were proud of, that said something about them.

It's possible to make your mark in many different ways, and we wanted to keep the brief open to see what would emerge. The results are weird and wonderful, warm, honest and funny stories, and we've been inspired by the people we've met.

Universal themes

The impetus for the project was the desire to discover what students believe and how they feel about the world of work and the journey they are about to embark on. What we found was that students are incredibly excited at the opportunities ahead of them, and what radiates throughout is their determination, resilience, stamina and excitement about the prospect of actually being able to make their mark.

Nurture and support are central to the ethos of the university, and students do feel nurtured and supported, but they know, too, that there are tough challenges ahead and they are fully aware of these. However, as well as their economic activity, among the many benefits they bring to the economy is their enthusiasm and willingness to continue learning. In every story and conversation you can feel the active engagement with the world of work and at the end of this collaborative project we are left feeling extremely optimistic about the future of these students in the workplace.

*****

Many people have helped this book become a reality and thanks go to Professor Judith Burnett, who had the vision to commission the project; Sheila Corrigan, her indefatigable PA; Abas Abow, an intern at the University of Greenwich, who not only wrote a story, but was an invaluable project administrator – he was always willing to help, which will stand him good stead on his own work journey; and the fantastic production team of editor, Lisa Hughes, and designer, Kate Ferruci.

However, most of all, thank you to the students, for showing up, for getting out their pens and writing, for sharing their thoughts, ideas and visual gifts. I am extremely confident they will be successful in making their mark in the world of work.

Dawn Reeves

May 2015

DANIELA LESKOVAR, MA STUDENT, ENGLISH:
LITERARY LONDON

Freedom

Focus.

Breathe in. Breathe out.

Empty your mind.

The sky is clear and the air is fresh. The conditions are perfect.

Calm down.

There are four kilometres of nothing below your feet, just a step away. A few birds in between perhaps. Yeah, don't forget the birds. And someone attached to you. Don't forget that either.

OK, I have to give in just for a second. Just hold the squeal. You can do flip-flops in your mind, but please do not squeal.

So yeah...

Oh my god!

I can't believe it!

This is insane! This is so insane! I seriously cannot believe it! I'm sky diving as a job! Look at the sky, and the clouds, and the air and the cold! I love the cold. These tiny crystals that appear on my nose are just so cute. And it's so funny when people keep sneezing afterwards. Oh, I love this! I so love this!

Now, calm down girl.

You've done this before. Billions of times. True, you weren't paid then, but now you're a professional, so show more seriousness and responsibility, and less crazy enthusiasm. Maybe these people don't love it yet, but they always love it once it's over. And get addicted. Like you did. Anyway, your job is to make people love sky diving. Love the fall. When they're at that stage between panicking and screaming with joy, you have to show them how to take control; how to ride the wind.

Now, concentrate. The sky is right there. All you need to do is embrace it and pull the others with you.

"Ready?" I ask. The girl attached to my front nods stiffly, forcing a small smile. She visibly pales and gulps in fear. A smile of encouragement is in place now. "Don't worry, it's fantastic." She giggles nervously, but prepares herself.

We glance over the edge. She grimaces. I grin.

The piercing scream is swallowed by the wind as soon as we push off and throw ourselves into freedom. ▶

Daniela Leskovar says:

My name is Daniela and I'm currently working on my Master's degree in English and literature at the University of Greenwich. I'm from Slovenia, a tiny country in southern Europe with lots of forests, mountains and a small piece of the sea. I moved to the UK in autumn 2014, having no idea what might wait for me in this foreign country. The reason I moved in the first place was to get the chance to make something more out of my writing hobby.

I have been working on my ideas regarding fiction stories for more than a decade. I started out as a fanfiction writer on different German and English web sites, struggling to combine my knowledge of the foreign language and my ideas. As a bookworm, I quickly walked into the world of fiction and even though not many have believed I could ever do something with my dream (I am not sure if it is a talent), I keep working hard to achieve the goal of publishing my first story in the form of a book.

The world of fiction has been part of my life since I knew how to read and I cannot imagine it not being part of my career. I have worked in different places, gaining knowledge and experience on my way to adulthood. This has given me more and more ideas about how to express what I feel and see; given me new perspectives on life; pushed me into imagining a possible future if I decided to stay in a particular position. It made me realize that the world is full of wonders yet to be discovered, and all one has to do is explore the possibilities, and use every opportunity that comes along to learn and gain something new, whether it is simple knowledge or long-lasting friendships and connections, which might make life more meaningful. ■

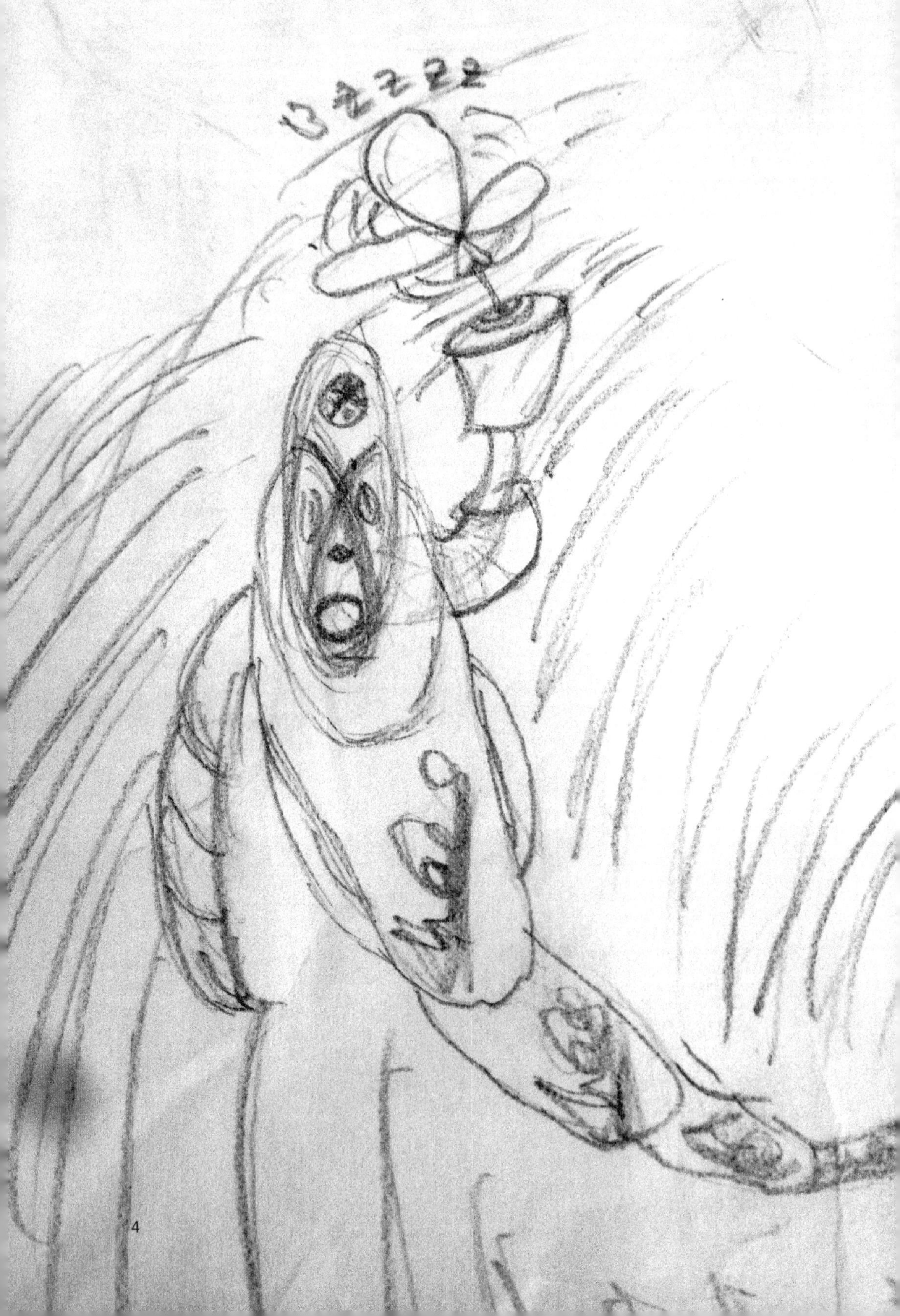

MOHAMMED SIDDIQUI, FIRST-YEAR STUDENT, MATHS

The X, Y, Z of it

"I stopped understanding maths the moment the alphabet decided to get involved." It's a meme I found on Twitter. It made me laugh, because even though I hate English, when the alphabet got involved that's when things started to take off for me. I love algebra. Pure maths, computing and modelling are also good, but algebra is great.

If I'm working on algebra I can find myself in a state of hyper-focus – totally into what I'm working on, not noticing what's happening in the world. Happy, actually. If it's a mathematical problem or subject I find easy, I doodle to help keep me focused. My favourite doodle is a Mexican masked worm. I don't know where it came from, but I like it and it's creative.

I'm lucky to have had inspiring teachers at school and here at uni and, although I don't think much about work yet, I'm positive about the future. One teacher has recommended that I go into actuarial work and I think modelling risk would be interesting.

I'm excited about the idea of helping people in a work situation and making friends, although I don't really expect work to be fun. I haven't got much work experience, but I've volunteered in a charity, helping them with their accounts system, and helped out with revision classes for younger students in school. I know the world of work isn't black and white and it takes time to find your way. I'm a reflective person, thoughtful maybe, but also a bit random sometimes.

In my dreams I'd love to be a rally driver. It's not realistic and, to be honest, I'm happy with driving cars on computer games. And because I'm into computing, I pushed the particle system as far as I could to get a more perfect picture and make it more authentic.

I don't really care about making a mark in the world of work. I suppose my personality and my approach to life – what I learned at home– is live to serve, make a positive contribution.

Here's another meme for you... "Sorry Maths, we can't find your X... she's not coming back and we don't know Y either...!" So if you want to find Y, just ask me! ∎

DANIELLE LAST, THIRD-YEAR STUDENT, GRAPHICS

Paper trail

A typewriter she bought at a car boot sale got Danielle to where she is now. It was a random purchase of a beautiful object, but the typewriter turned into a project. It made her think about typography and graphic design as a career. Danielle loves finding the narrative, a story that will engage, and her work always begin on paper. A piece of paper can start a conversation, she says.

As a student, Danielle has often stepped up to be project manager. She's not afraid of conflict and using her skills to reach a compromise between different people and their opinions. She would like to work in advertising and is keen to be involved in the whole process, building relationships and collaborating with others.

She has done two mobile development company internships, working on a mobile payment system and a waste management app. This was all good experience, but she is most proud of the 'brand book' she produced as part of her course. Hers is a handmade work of art, full of handwritten notes and stories, lovingly tied together.

Like many students coming to the end of their degree courses, Danielle is worried about not getting a job and not getting a job she enjoys, but she is excited about the prospect of getting her work out there, because she wants people to see what she can do. ∎

GEORGE HARVEY, THIRD-YEAR STUDENT,
CREATIVE WRITING

Never judge a book...

People who saw him must've thought he had the simplest job in the world; sitting down all day, beeping items and getting paid to do it. They must've thought he had no resolve to do anything better. But they were wrong.

They didn't know of the effort he put into getting up that morning. How he'd fought with his own body to get out of bed and silence his dreadful alarm clock.

Did they really think he enjoyed saying the same things over and over again, day after day, like a broken record? "Do you need help packing?" "Can I interest you in...?" And if he heard one more customer ask, "Can I have some more bags," he would...

You understand.

Anyone who thought his job was easy ought to try sitting – or standing – for hours, working like a machine, with every five minutes feeling like 50.

But he couldn't complain. He liked his job. Why wouldn't he? The pay was good and the hours were flexible, not to mention the travelling from here to home, which was easy. Plus, working helped him greatly with his social skills – he wasn't the hermit he used to be.

There were some friendly faces who appreciated his help and others who got angry and told him to shove their shopping up his... something. But they all saw him as a checkout operator; a young man who wouldn't achieve anything decent in life. They couldn't see beyond the till to his deeper skills or the fantasies that swam through his head or the things he'd already published, which they might've read themselves. They didn't know he exchanged emails with the very authors who wrote the books they were purchasing.

They were missing a great opportunity to ask for his autograph, because one day he would earn his living in a new way. The shelves would be stacked with books that had his name printed on them. Soon he'd shed his secret identity and expose his true powers to the world of writing. ▶

George Harvey says:

I am 20 years old and I am a third-year creative writing student with Asperger syndrome (autism). Since secondary school, I have been very passionate about writing, because a) I want to share my creative ideas with the world, and b) I want to make a difference. My dream is to one day create a successful children's book series, which gives motivation to others, and raises awareness of personal disabilities and issues, like autism.

In the past, I have written reviews for Amazon; posted several pieces of short fiction on writewords.org.uk; have contributed to Greenwich University's Latitude Lookout *magazine (with an interview that was posted online); and I have even been published with the National Autistic Society, and contributed to another book on Amazon called* Successful Studying.

My aim with the flash fiction I created for this book was to give something inspirational to readers. I wanted to show that even if a person has a disability, feels they're lacking in talent or are working in a low-rate job, they can still become successful in life. It's all a matter of having the right motivation and confidence to take the first steps. That's why my flash fiction is inspired by real-life events that happened to me, personally. (You could call it 'creative flash non-fiction'.)

I hope you enjoy my writing and that you take something beneficial from it. ■

SARAH WOLFIN, FIRST-YEAR STUDENT, MATHS

Calculated risk

Sarah has a fantastic drive to learn. She adores the mental stimulation of maths, being around people who love their subject and working together with other students.

She describes her 18-year-old self as too young for university. In fact, she dropped out the first time around, but always wondered whether she could really do the maths, so at the age of 55 she went back. It was a risk. She sold her house to pay the fees, but it's already been worth it. She finds Greenwich rejuvenating and recommends it to everyone, especially people who are getting older.

Perhaps more than most first-year students, Sarah has had her ups and downs. She's experienced redundancy and had to do soul-destroying jobs to keep afloat, but she says it's taught her to be resilient; to take the initiative and to make things happen.

Work is an important part of her identity. With a successful career in actuarial work, five years in the City managing a team of 20, plus teaching behind her, she isn't sure what she'll do next, but there are plenty of possibilities and that's what's really exciting.

For instance, she'd like to develop an app to teach times tables by setting them to music. It's the sort of thing she imagines working on with a few fellow students and sending out into the world. It's a great example of Sarah's 'why not?' approach.

She recognises that ageism can be an issue in some organisations, but ask her about making her mark and it's clear that her passion is to help raise the profile of women and education, and particularly women in maths. In fact, she is particularly proud of an article she wrote for the university magazine about Ada Lovelace, the early 19th century mathematician who worked with Charles Babbage and is often described as the world's first computer programmer. ■

SARA O'BRIEN, THIRD-YEAR STUDENT,
ENGLISH LITERATURE WITH CREATIVE WRITING

City street in the rain

She's hardly *Breakfast at Tiffany's*. Rather, she stands – a little hunched, a little tilted to the left, as if she cannot choose how to carry her weight – outside Gregg's. Their 99p sausage roll paired with a 99p cuppa, sipping on inspiration – perhaps a little too milky?

She sees diamonds, the city boys shimmering, slimeing into the street. The smog-filtered light makes sieving through the sterling from the plate a difficult task without a – pick-pocket? – loupe.

And the business girls, black and navy pencil skirts, stitched into office buildings, the same basting and hem throughout the university-educated circuit, a system. Somebody who knows somebody who knows somebody. They've filed themselves down to a synopsis, a repetition of words that hazard at hard working – bourgeois symbolism – built on pseudo-dreams.

Littered across the city – could they really be her age? – and everyone in a rush. Push. Past. Pause. Cigarette. Fast forward. Clicking in sync – 9,000 multiplied by three years and how many words per minute? – they pace to pace. She sees that some of them *believe* in the rush; noted, impaired and penciled in. The others manoeuvre through forgery; plain poker-faced, hollowed out insecurities. Keep – pretending? – moving!

Brogues and boots clack along to ticks and tacks, lunch hour, rush hour, after-hours, swept to a typist's slate. Observation through (coffee?) filtration, it starts to drizzle, spitting inconvenience into £5 cappuccinos.

She has never thought much about the rain, but she watches it liquefy the mobile cosmetic manifestations. They struggle out of – due to wet weather conditions take caution when choosing monotony – sensible shoes with the quickening speed of umbrella canopies and makeshift newspaper caps.

She has an involuntarily smirking reflex and indulges herself on the piteous glances. She's known to tuck them into her back pocket. She supposes it adds to the displacement. She leaves her tea on the side to collect pollutant drops and hobbles along. Jigsawing her directions, a few pieces soggy from the rain, she makes her way. A smudge or two of her own mascara deflates below her eyes – stuck and unstuck. ▶

Sarah O'Brien says:

The inspiration behind my story is moored in a place between my own uncertainty of post-university life and the confining nature of time, even in its indefinite progress. The in-between space that the story positions itself in reflects a portion of myself within the fictional, unnamed 'She'. The narrative generated around my real-time self, that of my three-year experience as an international student in London, is in a similar space, divided between two countries and continents.

My physical self and my mental self linger in limbo before an inevitable page conclusion and, from that, I write. My written piece combines this with a combination of vague impressions formed from people huddled in various business communities and their different strides around the city. How these strides can form a collective beat and image is what underlines my words.

As the story's first line suggests, I made a connection with Truman Capote's novella Breakfast at Tiffany's. *I admire Capote's concept of phoniness and I drew upon it through the city streets and within my protagonist herself. I aimed to portray the unconventional within the conventional and suggest the assimilation of the open, self-aware cynic.* ■

Europäisches
Patentamt

European
Patent Office

Office européen
des brevets

European Patent Office
80298 MUNICH
GERMANY

Questions about this communication ?
Contact Customer Services at www.epo.org/contact

Abdurrahman, Muhammad

Date	
	23.04.14

Reference	Application No./Patent No.
	14153939.5 - 1954
Applicant/Proprietor	
FUJITSU LIMITED	

Designation as Inventor - communication under Rule 19(3) EPC

You have been designated as inventor in the above-mentioned European patent application. Below you will find the data contained in the designation of inventor and further data mentioned in Rule 143(1) EPC:

DATE OF FILING : 05.02.14

PRIORITY : //

TITLE : Mesh quality improvement in computer aided engineering

DESIGNATED STATES : AL AT BE BG CH CY CZ DE DK EE ES FI FR GB GR HR HU IE IS IT LI LT LU LV MC MK MT NL NO PL PT RO RS SE SI SK SM TR

INVENTOR (PUBLISHED = 1, NOT PUBLISHED = 0):

1/Georgescu, Serban/
1/Chow, Peter/
1/Kubota, Tetsuyuki/
1/Abdurrahman, Muhammad/
1/Sakairi, Makoto/

DECLARATION UNDER ARTICLE 81 EPC:
The applicant(s) has (have) acquired the right to the European patent as employer(s).

Receiving Section

MUHAMMED ABDURRAHMAN, FOURTH-YEAR
STUDENT, SOFTWARE ENGINEERING

Patent pending

It's a fantastic achievement for an intern to have filed not one but two patents for innovative software development. Fujitsu, the company employing Muhammed on placement in their R&D lab, were so impressed by the contribution he was able to make that they gave him a bonus. During an amazing year out, Muhammed also delivered a paper at the International Association of the Engineering Modelling, Analysis and Simulation Community conference.

Being in a close knit community of 40 researchers suited him. People relied on each other to help them complete their tasks, but it was a highly organised environment with a clear structure and it worked. The culture was quite formal and reserved, but it taught Muhammed how to interact with colleagues in a respectful way.

One of the biggest success factors for Muhammed was the input of his mentor at Futjitsu, Dr Peter Chow, who took time each month to talk to him, helping him settle in and showing concern for his well-being. Dr Chow had previously been a student at Greenwich, which made a big difference.

Muhammed is about to finish uni and has already been offered a software engineering job, but he's still considering his next move. Should he apply for a PhD or get some more industry experience first? Just now he's finding it hard to make the right decision, but he admits it's a great position to be in. ▪

JULIA SKOWRONSKA, THIRD-YEAR STUDENT,
ENGLISH LITERATURE AND CREATIVE WRITING

Where a thousand paper cranes fly

The anxiety drifted at her shoulders like a ghost. She kept her face calm, but she couldn't relax her back and her neck was stiff.

She heard footsteps in the corridor. Male voices. She swallowed, fighting the lump in her throat. Her heart hammered against her ribcage. She took more air, but it didn't seem like enough.

Two men entered the meeting room. David was a sharp man in his fifties. He was the film producer. She hadn't had the chance to meet the other man face to face yet. They'd been in the same building three times, but he never knew. He probably had no idea who she was until recently.

To her, he was everything, though. He was the man who inspired her words; those words that made it onto the paper and sold across the world. This man was the biggest influence on her work. His music wasn't just any music. It was universes; it was art; it was unimaginable beauty. It has been her biggest dream to meet him and to be able to tell him that.

"Meet Hans Zimmer. He's our composer," said David.

Mr Zimmer smiled brightly and held out his hand. His hair already greyed, although he wasn't sixty yet.

"Pleasure to meet you, Miss Carter," he said. "I've read your book. I'm a big fan."

She shook his hand absently, trying to make words from the chaos inside her head. She had so much to say to him. She was so grateful. This book wouldn't exist without him.

She smiled as they let go. "Likewise. I'm happy we'll work together."

"Wonderful," said David. "Let's sit down and start. Coffee, anyone?"

She was quiet in the meeting, unable to put into words what she wanted to say to him. But maybe he knew.

Maybe he saw it in her eyes. Besides, what could she really say? Meeting him meant she was where she had always wanted to be. They were both artists whom people loved. They were equals. And even though she couldn't find the courage to openly talk to him, they both knew they'd made it. ▶

Julia Skrowronska says:

I am a university student who loves to travel, meditate and sketch. I hope to become a novelist one day. The story was inspired by my dream of meeting my favourite composer, Hans Zimmer, a man who has a major influence on my writing. ■

KELVEN BARBOSA, SECOND-YEAR STUDENT,
3D DESIGN AND DIGITAL ANIMATION

Animated discussion

Kelven can deal with stress. He knows how to keep focused and manage his time. He's learnt this through working at McDonald's for the last four years. He's now a manager, with the added responsibilities that brings, but luckily he's highly self-motivated and the hours are flexible, so work has actually become easier.

Kelven admits he can be quite competitive, but he feels he's had to be. Getting into university in the first place was tough – having taken a BTEC route, he had to get double distinctions to earn enough UCAS points – and he came to the UK relatively recently, from Mozambique via Portugal, so he's constantly had to make cultural adjustments.

When he talks about what led him to study 3D design and digital animation, he immediately goes back to Disney cartoons. He wants to share the enjoyment he experienced watching films as a child. Kelven loves to laugh and he wants to share his sense of fun, to engage an audience. For many of his peers, the focus is purely on the action, but Kelven cares about the story, whatever the genre.

His career plan involves developing a group with fellow students to create animations that showcase their talents, working freelance and hopefully getting a job doing 3D modelling for a games company like Rockstar. His 3D rendered centaur is an example of his work.

To make his mark in the world of animation would be fantastic and maybe, just maybe, he might do some acting, too. He likes to challenge himself and normally sets himself achievable targets, but, he says, you never know! ∎

ABDUL MUTABBIR, FIRST-YEAR STUDENT, MATHS

Making experience count

There have been two great moments in my life. The best day was at Hoxton Hall. I took part in a community arts project called Hipnotic. The graffiti workshop was held by Tizer and Shucks from ID Crew and it brought together graffiti artists, breakdancers, different crews, people inspired by New York subway art. The picture shows a grafitti wall I helped create as part of the project. I felt totally alive, really fulfilled. We learned teamwork and it felt like being in a family. It didn't matter if you made a mess. I'd never taken part in anything like it.

The second experience was working at the Olympics and Paralympics in 2012. That completely opened my eyes. I was working in the Copper Box venue, where they had goalball, a team sport for blind athletes. It was a great experience and I saved money to pay my fees. My family moved from Telford, a small town in the Midlands, to London, so I appreciated the diversity.

Before I came to Greenwich I was studying pharmacy, but I failed my second year. I don't want to be the kind of person who says, 'If only I'd done this...' so I decided to jump to maths. I had to be persistent. It was important for me and my family. My mum kept me going. I know she really cares about what happens to me, so I had to go for it.

I used to be a shy person, but I'm not worried about peer group pressure anymore. I'm still scared of failing – the exam thing was a big shock – but I'm not scared to tell anyone about it. It's human to make mistakes. You reflect, learn and become something different.

I'm inspired by my maths course. I'm interested in data analysis, operational research, using analytical tools and applying maths. The lecturers have linked me into the Institute of Maths and its Applications, and I've been involved with some great events – a session with University College London (UCL), a Transport for London (TfL) simulation, and I was successful in becoming an outreach science, technology, engineering and maths (STEM) ambassador.

I'm not sure exactly what I want to do in future. Work in the Civil Service maybe? Somewhere I can move around, get experience, carry on learning and make a difference. Being seen as a positive, good, hard-working person is important to me. I want to be like the inspiring people I've met along the way so far. I'm excited about the prospect of coming home from work with a smile on my face. ■

MATHURA BALANADARASAN, MSC STUDENT,
BUSINESS AND FINANCIAL ECONOMICS

High hopes

It was Monday morning and she rushed up the escalators in her heels. When she emerged from the station she stood there, taking in the skyscrapers of Canary Wharf, home to some of the tallest buildings in the city and London's financial district.

One building in particular caught her eye. It was the square-shaped glass tower at 25 Bank Street. She craned her neck. The company's name was in the top left-hand corner. She took a deep breath and read that name: JP Morgan.

Someone behind her was talking about financial trading. She turned her head slightly and saw two men in dark suits. She recognised them as students who had been to the assessment day with her. She greeted them and joined their conversation. They talked about the questions they might be asked in their final interview for the internship at JP Morgan.

When they reached the entrance to the building she stopped. One of her new-found friends asked what was she smiling at. This is the building, she told him, that I have walked past for the last four years. Every time I walked past I thought about how cool it would be to get a job in this company and here I am on its threshold. She pushed her shoulders back and stepped in... ▶

Mathura Balanadarasan says:

I am an MSc business and financial economics student at the University of Greenwich. On completion of my course I would like to start working in investment banking and the story I have written was inspired by the real stories of many economics students. We all want to work in the city, but the competition is exceptionally high and the application process is very long. ■

RITA KUCINSKAITE, THIRD-YEAR STUDENT,
GRAPHIC DESIGN

Sound and vision

Rita's focus is the moving image and how it's used in the creative industries, particularly advertising and marketing. This comes from being really into film – she describes herself as a film maniac and a music lover. She loves classic horror, *Rosemary's Baby*, *Schindler's List*, *The Piano* and *1984*, but it's always about the subject of the film, the issues explored, not the genre. At the heart of it for Rita are moving images that stay with you.

As a child she was always making videos, using the family camera as her tool and family holidays as her subject. She experimented with arranging footage and sound, noticing that syncing sound with visuals made her more involved with the scenes.

What excites her about her creative work (see the still from a music video she made, which she's very proud of) is how emotional connections with film and visual material can help change opinions. She can apply that to her professional work in advertising, but also for social good. She believes in social justice and equality, and hates corruption, war for bad reasons and exploitation. If the film and images she produces capture people's imagination and make them stay with an idea or a feeling, think about it twice, she's happy.

Her ideal is to work in a small creative agency, a collaborative team environment, and in the run-up to the end of her final year Rita is already freelancing, using her design skills working with a property asset management company. It's already got decent branding, but she's been tasked with making improvements and a corporate video. She's earning money and enjoying the work.

She says she's worried about everything about the world of work, that judgements are hard and she won't be good enough. She feels that the gap between uni and the world of work is huge, but the freelancing is helping that and her tutors have been great. Making a mark for Rita is about conveying a message successfully and helping people's voices to be heard. ■

ELLIE DAVIES, FOURTH-YEAR STUDENT,
BUSINESS INFORMATION SYSTEMS

Impact statement

Ellie spent her placement year working as an integration analyst in a digital marketing department at an IT company. It was a positive experience, definitely fun in parts, and clients included famous names such as John Lewis and Asos. She learnt about sticking up for herself and the need for stamina – working overtime was commonplace – but she says she did find it hard to make an impact as a young woman in an environment where she felt women weren't valued as highly as men.

She says she did encounter sexism, but had the self-confidence to take that aspect of the world of work in her stride. She puts this down to the positive role models she's had, from the female university tutors who have worked in the IT industry to a particular A level teacher who believed in her and encouraged her to keep going.

Her family have always been very supportive, too, and Ellie herself has had to work to overcome dyslexia. However, she says the way her brain works sometimes means she has an advantage and can see solutions or patterns that others can't.

Back in college after her year out in industry, she can't wait to get a job again. She'd like to work in a corporate organisation, but expects it to be hard to find a position that combines IT and business, although that's the focus of her degree.

Since the placement she's thought a lot about quality of life versus money. She isn't afraid of hard work, but she doesn't want to achieve success by spending all hours and every weekend at the office. She wants to make a mark by being herself and using her people skills to make a difference. One day perhaps she'll be an ambassador for a charity. ■

SID JOSHI, ALUMNUS,
SOFTWARE ENGINEERING

Above and beyond

"I always tell students they need to go above and beyond what's expected. Give more than a hundred per cent. Don't just study what's on the curriculum, think about the latest industry trends as well as what interests you the most. What would make you stand out? That's what I did." For the students who are fortunate enough to be mentored by Sid, he is proof that his approach works.

Sid is a successful alumnus of Greenwich University. He graduated in 2005 and received a first-class honours degree in software engineering. He went to work for a small IT company, where he gained a wide range of experience in IT, including programming, networking, solutions design and support. A year later he moved to a consulting role with BEA Systems, which was later acquired by Oracle.

Sid's current role at Oracle is as a Senior Principal Consultant. "I love my job – the variety of projects, the customers, the challenges, solving enterprise problems, delivering success-ful projects," he says. He is passionate about his work and has received several awards for going above and beyond the call of duty. Sid is keen to progress his career further within Oracle and looks forward to new challenges.

A shy but naturally curious child, at nine he saw his first computer, in his dad's workplace, and was fascinated by it. His curiosity grew ever more over the years and even now he has the same passion about learning new technologies and keeping up with industry trends.

For Sid, making your mark is about making a success of whatever you do by applying yourself and seeing it through to the end. He's certainly an inspiration to the students he mentors. ■

MACKSON EJEJIGBE, MSC STUDENT,
COMPUTING AND INFORMATION SYSTEMS

A passion for change

Temisan was from a humble background, his dad a primary school teacher and his mum a tailor. He was from the south-south region of Nigeria, the hub of Nigeria's economy.

One would expect life to be easy as a result of the oil and gas, but the reverse was the case. The environment was polluted. The people could not fish and they had no clean drinking water.

As Temisan walked along the street he saw his childhood friend, Tosan, who happened to be a first-class graduate. They got talking and Tosan told him that he had been searching for a job for the past five years, but all to no avail.

As they walked, Temisan saw dilapidated buildings and malnourished children crying. He saw youths roaming the streets. He saw corruption and strikes. He saw the spread of malaria, HIV/AIDs and Ebola.

Temisan shouted out to the top of his voice, "Oh Africa! My beloved continent! Why are we suffering?"

Due to Temisan's passion and desire to help, he decided to form a revolutionary army. He would equip himself with the requisite skills and knowledge to build networks to face the challenges of tomorrow.

After graduating from law school, he founded the African Legal, Industrial and Economic Forum. He put smiles on the faces of people and restored hope, joy and dignity.

At exactly 7am, in the early hours of 4 November, Tosan woke up, washed his face and went straight to his friend's house to relate his dream. "Temisan! Temisan! Open the door! I have good news for you."

Temisan reluctantly opened the door, because he was still enjoying the early morning breeze hushing in from his window. Tosan enthusiastically narrated his dream to Temisan,

"I slept last night and I saw in my dream an Africa that is completely different from what we have now – a continent where there is justice and fairness, equal rights and integrity, social welfare for all, quality infrastructure, proper service delivery and a vibrant economy."

Tosan's narrative rekindled Temisan's passion and zeal for Africa. Today Temisan is blazing a trail and he is a success and a force to reckon with any time, any day. ▶

Mackson Ejejigbe says:

I hail from Warri, Delta State, Nigeria. I graduated from the Federal University of Technology, Minna, Nigeria, with a B.Tech degree in information technology and am currently doing a Masters degree in computing and information systems (finishing in September 2015). I am passionate about the young people of Africa and am determined to help create jobs and make life better for African youth. My motivation for taking part in this project was to be able to tell the story of what young people are facing in Africa and to send a message of hope for a better Africa. ■

MATILDA BINERI, FIRST-YEAR STUDENT, MATHS

Soul food

I came alone to the UK from Albania via Italy. I worked hard, became a chef, got married, had a daughter and now I study maths at Greenwich! I knew I could survive without a degree, but I didn't want to go through life with any regrets.

I love to cook, to feed and nurture people, and I love numbers. Being good with numbers helped me as a chef. It still does. I've worked for the same restaurant company for six years and now I'm training new chefs, supporting their development and updating courses for them. When I told my employers I wanted to work part-time and study at university they were fine with it, although I don't think they could really believe I wanted to study maths.

What's important to me is to be a role model for my daughter. I've got a brain and I'm going to use it! I want her to know that everything is possible. I was worried about going back into education at the age of 34, but I've been amazed by the inspiring lecturers who are so willing to help; the resources available. The UK is more of a meritocracy than other countries. It's so open. I'm already imagining my graduation ceremony in a couple of years. I will bring the whole family, but especially my mum.

A degree is a passport to a better future. When I started the course I thought I'd go into teaching maths to teenagers, because I'm good with young people, but already I'm thinking bigger. Maybe I'll work in the finance sector? I enjoy calculating risk and problem-solving.

I'm not sure some of the younger students appreciate the gap there is between school or university and going into work, so more contact with the world of work would be good, and even though I'm lucky to have an income, the fees make it tough for all of us.

My maths heroes are Einstein and Newton, and I like to visit Madame Tussauds in different cities and take photos of their waxworks (you can see one of my pictures opposite!). I'd like to make my mark by inventing something, bringing something unique to the world and leaving something good behind. ■

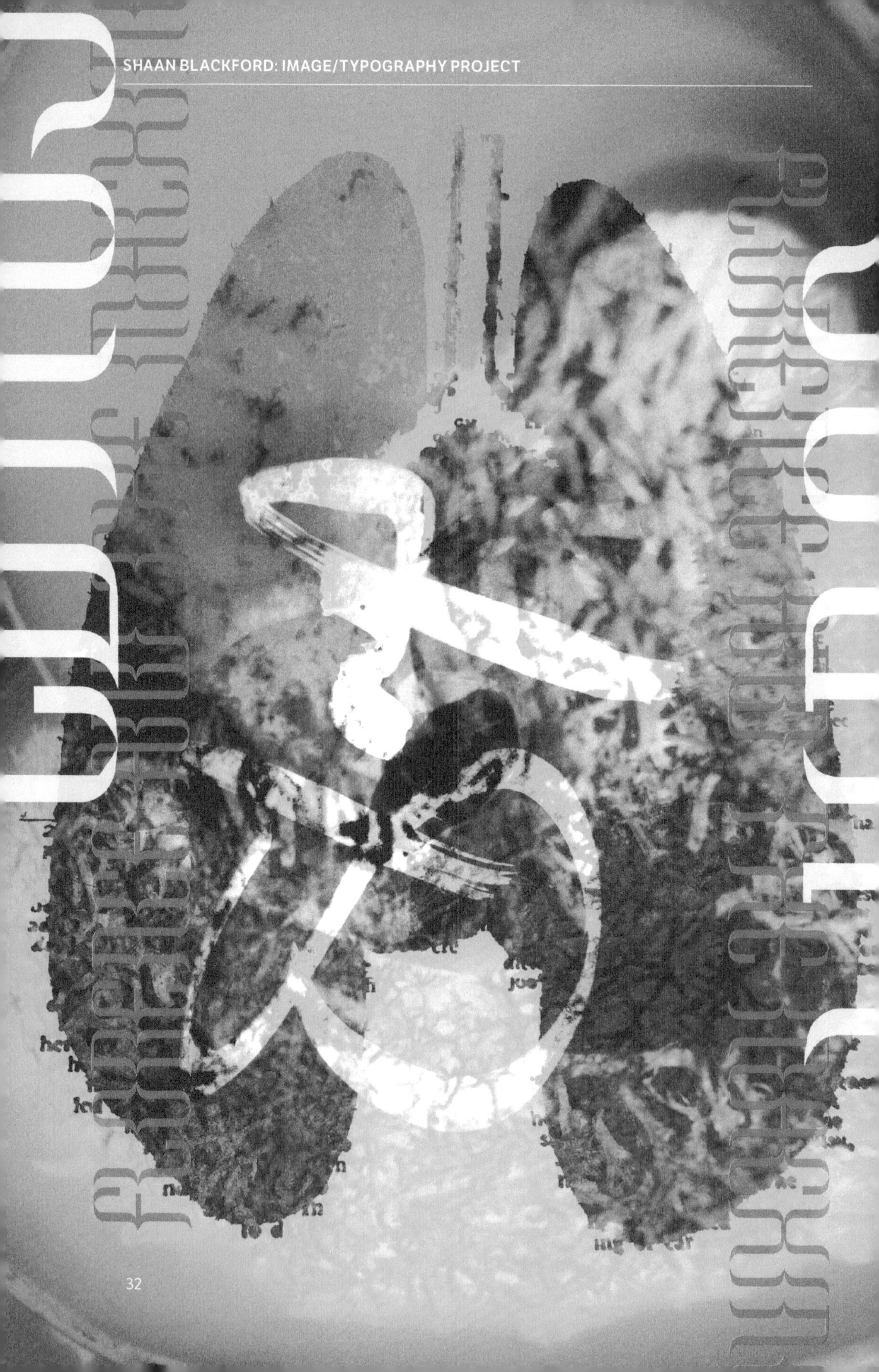

SHAAN BLACKFORD, THIRD-YEAR STUDENT,
GRAPHIC DESIGN

Creative line of enquiry

I'm a designer, but I spend lots of time in the library. I stay up all night reading, researching every possibility, until the deadline is right up on me and I have to make it happen. That kind of stress and pressure is good, and my designs seem to come out well, but it can be a rollercoaster.

I suppose that's why I find it hard to say what I want to do in the future. I'm not ready to be tied down. I like to do a bit of everything. My nan and I used to go round craft fairs together when I was young. I loved pulling lots of different techniques, materials and colours together. I was lucky that any hobby I had growing up – and trust me I tried a lot – I always had support at home.

I like the idea of becoming an art director in an advertising company, because it brings all the elements of design into one place, although for now I'm interested in doing a masters degree. I can be quite academic and I'm interested in the philosophy of aesthetics and beauty. I guess it's about finding my own line of enquiry, my own way.

I work during the holidays and outside college, but it's not a graduate job. I worry about starting at the bottom of another ladder in the graphics industry, but I'm excited about the new things I could learn and new challenges, the possibility of becoming a success. It's hard for me to answer the question about making my mark. I'm always too unsure of the next few steps, right until the final minute, so I can't say.

I'm proud of my image/typography project. It's a collection of posters and I love the results. I suppose it's like life – I guess I just have to trust myself and it will all come together in the end. ■

HANNE NORD, FIRST-YEAR STUDENT,
CREATIVE WRITING

Flickering faith

I know I'm good. And I'm also aware that makes me sound arrogant, but the truth is simply that I am, in fact, excellent at what I do. My only problem is that the right people don't know how good I am. Yet.

Writing has always been my passion and I'm a sucker for good movies. The day I discovered it was possible to work as a screenwriter was the day I knew what to do with the rest of my life.

From that point onwards I've been chipping off my bad writing habits and polishing up the good parts into a sculpture that I'm ready to show off.

My most recent statue is the screenplay that will make the right people recognise my talent – only for it to be broken into pieces and glued back together by some eccentric director, because that's the truth about this business, I know, but my work will still be up on that pedestal.

"We will be in touch with you shortly," said the coltish man with the too-small suit and the weirdly shaped and no doubt expensive sunglasses. He seemed genuine, so I coughed up my most charming smile before extending my hand.

My hopes were high this time, so I fumbled through my thoughts for a fitting reply. I needed to present myself as sure, positive, but still humble. "Thank you, I look forward to working with you."

Letting go of the man's hand, a hand that had surprisingly been sweatier than mine, I felt a burst of confidence. He smiled at me. This had to be it! But then again I'd learned, the hard way, not to hope too much, because it makes the disappointing blow much harder to take, the stinging bruise of shame more difficult to wear.

I shook the rest of the right hands in the room and left, head held high. As soon as I got out of the building I let my mask drop and, although I am a non-believer, looked to the sky. ▶

Hanne Nord says:

I am from Bergen, Norway. I'm studying in London because I want to meet people, experience different cultures and see the world – and London is such a great place to begin my adventures! When I started my creative writing degree in September last year I thought I wanted to write novels, but after a few months of trying out different things I think I want to be a screenwriter too! That would be the perfect thing to do considering my love for film.

The idea for my piece came from stories I've heard about how hard it is to break into the film industry as a screenwriter, and the fact that you have to really know your craft to succeed at it. I thought about how you would have to present yourself to producers and directors as very certain of yourself to make a good impression, but how hard that would be for me, especially if someone had given my work a definite 'no' previously. So I thought I'd write a story that would lead the reader to perceive the narrator in a certain way at the beginning and then add a twist to that at the end. ■

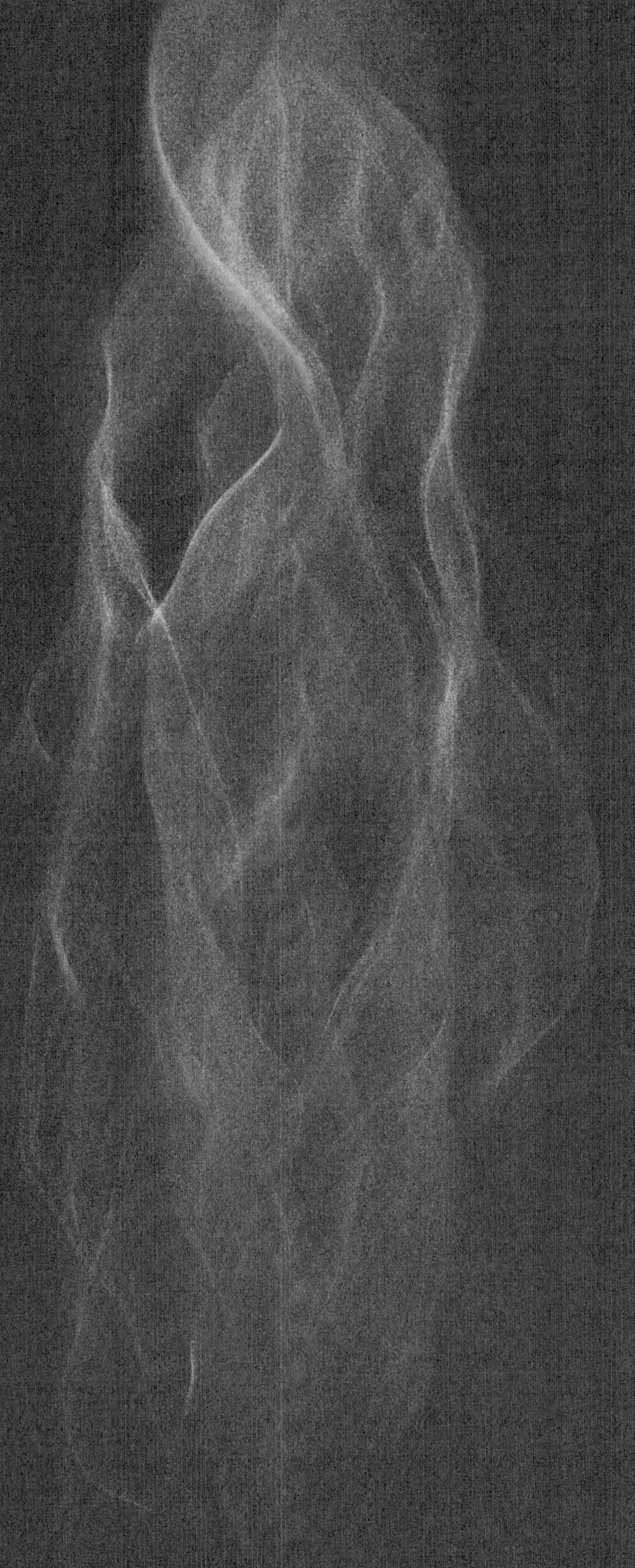

ALEKS SKUDNEVS, FIRST-YEAR STUDENT,
3D DESIGN

Fifth dimension

"I see the world like a blueprint," says Aleks. He takes his inspiration from computer games and likes to immerse himself in a complete world. He finds himself focusing on what's different about a game, picking out the aspects that aren't standard and then developing them as far as he can, testing and modelling different alternatives with software. "What's important is to make it yourself," he asserts.

When he was at school Aleks had an admin role, which taught him about team work, but he doesn't have much formal work experience. He's now looking for a part-time job, maybe some freelancing, and one good thing he did recently was modelling a sauna in 3D. The opportunity came to him by chance, but he got paid for his work and enjoyed it.

Thinking ahead about what worries him about work, Aleks highlights the difficulty of selling himself, and the fact that he'll have a big debt when he leaves college. It would be exciting to work in a 3D games environment, but it's hard to know where to start and he would appreciate as much help from the university as possible.

However, Aleks is proud of the work he's done to simulate fire in 3D and his imagination is sparked by all sorts of future possibilities, as demonstrated in the image shown here entitled 'What you see is 4.600.000 particles turbulently flowing in one direction'.

One example he gives involves what could be done with holograms – he's seen some amazing possibilities in Chicago and talks animatedly about how 3D sensors could scan in a person and send them via a hologram to New York. "Maybe I'll make my mark in 5D," he smiles. ■

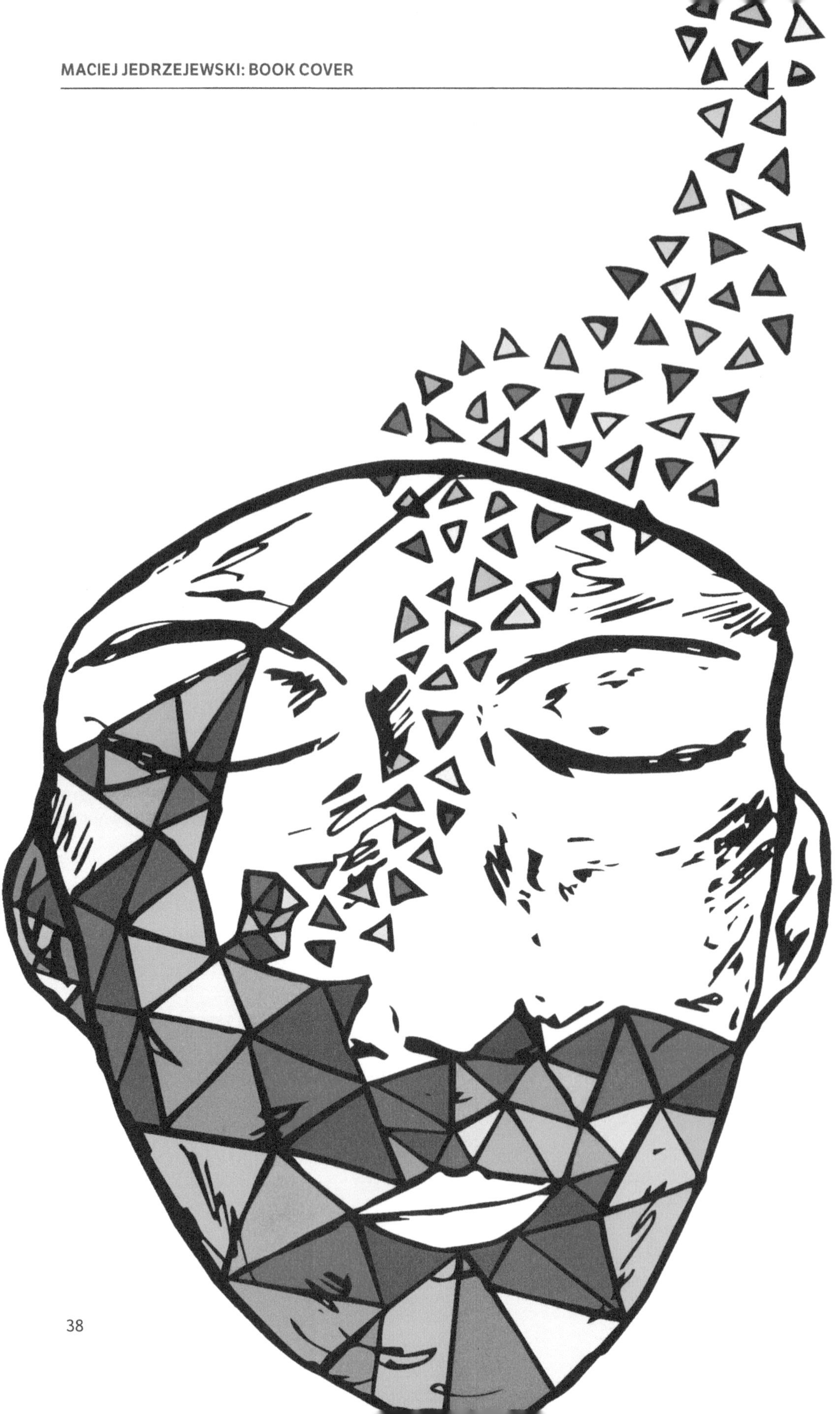

MACIEJ JEDRZEJEWSKI, THIRD-YEAR STUDENT,
GRAPHICS

Better by design

Maciej's family say that as a child he was desperate to draw what was in his head. When those images were inspired by dreams, he would wake up in the middle of the night and, finding no paper, begin drawing on his bedroom walls, including abstract creatures and random shapes.

He describes himself as someone who's all about creating light and mood, and exploring colour, but he also considers himself a professional. "If you think 'I'm a professional' you are. It's about having a professional approach and doing things properly." He's already been part of a start-up graphics company and has worked for a range of clients in the music and video industries.

He knows he has a design style that's recognisably his own – see the image used on the front of this publication – and hopes the industry will be open-minded about new approaches. However, he acknowledges, "You have to learn it all: how to work with clients, take people's needs and feelings into account, how to approach the job, plan it, work out how much time it will take, what to charge, how to promote yourself – everything."

Maciej is full of energy, hungry for a job and excited by the opportunities available in the capital. "London is the city of graphic design and I believe design can make it a better place for everyone," he concludes. ■

CHIZENG DUONG, SECOND-YEAR STUDENT,
ENGLISH LITERATURE

Unexpected incident

I'm in an unrecognisable place. I can't get up. I am cold, still and alone. I am frozen. I feel disconnected. I am trapped.

"Please wake up."

I feel a warm hand on my icy one. I long to reach out and give it a reassuring squeeze, but I just can't move. My body rejects movement.

"Please wake up. I'm sorry for what happened. Everyone at work will miss you. We don't want to lose you."

I scream mentally, "Help me! Take me home!" Her voice seems to fade as I drift off once again to flashback...

How could I be so stupid as to trust her? I storm out of the office in distress. I run blindly into the road, narrowly missing the cars which roar by, beeping constantly. I continue to run when suddenly a hard object hits me at speed, sending me flying over the bonnet and straight onto the concrete. Piercing screams follow.

"Please, if you can hear me open your eyes and speak to me. I am so sorry. I am right here."

I try as hard as I can to respond to her pleading. I long to reach out so much, to hold her hand, but I cannot. My body is being controlled, possessed.

Sobs and tears, a few shifts and shuffles, a kiss goodbye on the forehead and her voice is gone again.

Painstakingly, agonisingly exhausted, I try one last time. "Please... someone help me." There is no one there. ▶

Chizeng Duong says:

I'm Chizeng. I am currently in my second year studying English literature and, like my character, I have dreams of a career in publishing and know that in order to get into this industry I will have to work hard and focus on my studies. However, there are many setbacks in life and whatever journey we take giving up is not an option, but, to achieve your goals, learning and improving is the way forward.

My story was inspired by dreams I have had since childhood. As we reach adulthood these dreams seem to be more reachable. However, these dreams and ambitions can suddenly be taken away from you due to a single careless encounter, and this is what I wanted to present in my short piece: life seems to be going fine one moment then the next it seems time moves on, but you remain frozen and helpless. ■

LEWIS HATFULL, THIRD-YEAR STUDENT,
3D DESIGN AND ANIMATION

Taking a (second) chance

Before this course I was studying architecture. I still have a strong passion for architecture. However, 3D is now my new path and I'm pleased I chose it.

Previously, before going back to my studies, I was working in a hotel for a year. It turned out to be a good thing. I learnt the business, worked hard and was rewarded with a promotion to a managerial position.

However, aside from the hotel, I have always loved art and design, and when I was talking to colleagues, friends and family, I knew I wanted to go back to university. I took it upon myself to get in contact with the university to see if this was possible. It felt like a risk, applying to come back, considering my experience before, but it was fantastic when a tutor suggested the 3D course, between them and the architecture school they sorted it out.

Coming back to university again I have noticed the difference in myself. I am more focused, I manage my time far more efficiently and I am far more proactive. I am here to improve.

In terms of a career, I am open to all opportunities in 3D, but I'm particularly interested in being a 3D visualizer for a large architecture practice. I follow companies that I would like to be a part of, such as BIG, a really innovative Danish architecture company, Fosters and Partners, and Milk.

I know I need something unique in my portfolio (see my textured 3D creature image), because expectations in the design world are so high, but I'd love a company to appreciate my designs, the blood, sweat and tears that goes into them, to see that I have an eye for quality, and to notice there is a story behind each piece of work. ■

DEBORAH REILLY, SECOND-YEAR STUDENT,
ENGLISH LITERATURE

It wasn't me

Dear Diary, I'm so excited to be here. This is the first day of forever. I'm going to be a model employee, get noticed by my boss and progress...

Six years later, I laugh at my naivety. Oh how wrong I was!

Six years later, I'm still a 'paper-pusher'. I can count how many people know my name, but have lost count of how many know me as 'Coffee Girl'. I'm miserable, but the wage keeps me here. As long as there's food in the fridge and a roof over my head that's all that matters, right?

I usually go to bed and wake up in a terrible mood. However, today was different. I felt more positive. I don't like this feeling.

I took my time dressing, defrosted the car and left. I walked through the front door of the office and a crowd was gathered. Once they noticed me a path opened up. I try to avoid crowds like the plague.

"Everyone, I'd like to introduce you to my new assistant, Katie," a voice boomed. The owner of the voice put his hand on my shoulder. Some clapped, most muttered. I just looked at my feet in shame. It wouldn't take him long to realise that he'd got the wrong person.

An hour later I decided to bring it up with him. "No, you've been here a long time. I've watched you for a while," he said, grinning like a Cheshire Cat. What was he up to? "Trust him," my head screamed. And I did.

We quickly settled into a routine. I'd bring him his breakfast and coffee each morning before we met the clients. I was becoming known. I even had a few friends now.

Then money started to evaporate from the company. But where was it going? I found the paperwork as the police walked through the front door.

My name, my signature, my identity was all over those documents. I was quickly hand-cuffed and taken away, while he stood there grinning, yet shaking his head.

I had been framed. I was convicted for a crime that I didn't commit. It upset me when no one knew my name. If only I could go back... ▶

Deborah Reilly says:

I am a 22-year-old, second-year English literature student at the University of Greenwich. I decided to participate in this project on a whim – and it is one of the best things that I have done as it has enabled my creative side to shine through.

I am a film fanatic and watching a film about swindling money from a company inspired my flash fiction, as I wanted to explore the side of the innocent party, instead of the villain's side. In the future, I wish to travel around the globe teaching English as a foreign language before settling down and teaching within a school. ∎

LIZZIE LENNON, THIRD-YEAR STUDENT,
GRAPHICS

Be happy

Are you happy with where you are? That's one question I don't want to be asking myself in five years' time. It's important to me that wherever I end up in my career I am happy.

I have two passions: advertising and marketing, and as a hobby pattern design (see my fruit and vegetable wallpaper – it's called '5 a day in a different way'). I have previously gained work experience at a large advertising and marketing agency, and I am due to go back to gain further experience in the coming months. The experience showed me that this is the career path I want to take. My expectations of a stressful environment were quickly changed, as it was a very supportive, happy and calm work environment.

Getting my voice heard is important to me as I believe every idea is important and not to be missed. I know that can be hard, but I'm pretty determined. I've learned to manage my emotions, keep my feet on the ground and stay open to feedback. You can't crumble.

I wish I could know everything there is to know about graphic design and advertising, but that will only come with experience. I guess that's what keeps me pushing myself to learn. I don't think you will ever know everything there is to know, but it's worth a try.

My goal is to have an idea of mine go global, build up a good reputation in the industry and make my mark. And don't forget to smile! ▄

NUSRATH AHMED, INTERN

Final reckoning

The menacing figure was motionless.

Tom stared into the dreary, foreboding eyes of his executioner, his hands trembling, a thin layer of sweat forming at his brow.

The noise of the ticking clocked pierced the silent atmosphere as every second passed at the pace of a snail.

Today would've been a normal day for Tom, a normal guy with a normal life. He had left his family at home and desperately hoped to go back to them, to see happiness in their eyes, to see their smiles, to hear their laughter.

He had known this day would come soon and had always tried to prepare himself, but it had arrived without him even realising and now he was trapped.

A sharp glint in the eyes of the figure marked a change of expression. He slowly moved towards Tom. Time appeared to slow further.

Was the figure coming closer or was the room getting smaller? Tom's heartbeat echoed around the space, his blood roaring in his ears, his face hot, chills running down his spine. The figure was almost upon him now. "Is this it?" he thought.

Images of his wife and his one-year-old son flashed through his head. "I won't give up," he told himself, mustering every ounce of courage as the figure approached, a hand reaching out.

"Tom, would you like to come in? Your interview will begin shortly." ▶

Nusrath Ahmed says:

I have been working as an intern at the university, having completed an MSc in business and financial economics. Working with university students I have understood that even the most confident students underestimate themselves when it comes to applying for jobs and attending interviews, and students were my inspiration! ■

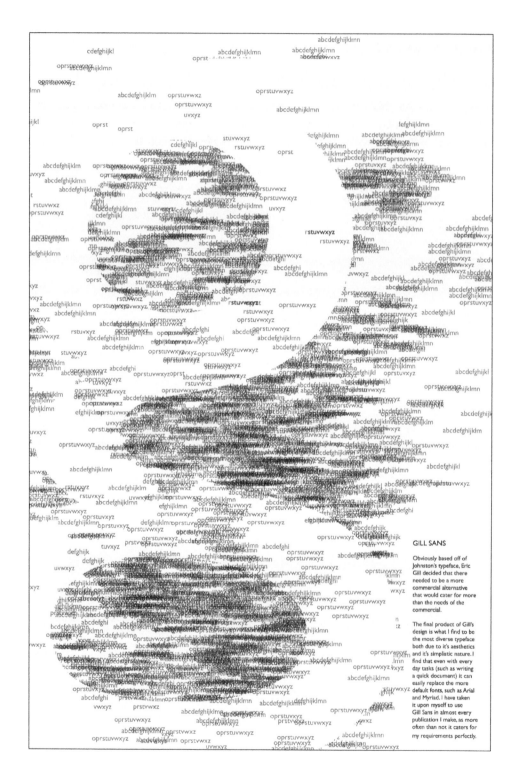

GILL SANS

Obviously based off of Johnston's typeface, Eric Gill decided that there needed to be a more commercial alternative that would cater for more than the needs of the commercial.

The final product of Gill's design is what I find to be the most diverse typeface both due to it's aesthetics and it's simplistic nature. I find that even with every day tasks (such as writing a quick document) it can easily replace the more default fonts, such as Arial and Myriad. I have taken it upon myself to use Gill Sans in almost every publication I make, as more often than not it caters for my requirements perfectly.

JOSHUA PRICE, FIRST-YEAR STUDENT,
GRAPHIC DESIGN

Search for satisfaction

I've previously worked in catering, which I go back to whenever I'm on holiday from university. I have also undertaken freelance work by assisting a family friend with his graphic design business.

I've always aspired to be a designer for an independent firm. However, I've recently realised how rewarding working in secondary education would be. If I did that I would choose a typically 'underprivileged' school and aim to work in Kent, my home county, as I understand how the education system works there. The obvious teaching specialisation for me would be either graphic design or art, as that's what I'm most interested in and knowledgeable about.

What excites me most is how satisfied I could feel at the end of the day. My main goal is to feel that I have helped someone, or a group of people, as it would make for a much more enjoyable experience day-in, day-out.

Although I am currently only a first-year student, I feel I need a better understanding of what happens with work experience, what it's like out in the field. I've been told that you find out more in the second and third year, but at the moment I don't know what a real design brief feels like.

I'd like to make my mark by sharing knowledge and helping other people get where they want to be. I've spent time and money on my education and I don't see why I should keep that to myself. ■

SHAKELA BEGUM, FIRST-YEAR STUDENT,
ENGLISH LITERATURE AND CREATIVE WRITING

Message from the author (a draft)

Procrastination is spending years 'perfecting' my craft, dwelling on life and obtaining a degree.

Hi, I'm Carina ~~and this is my novel~~.

(OK, no author writes that, let alone says it out loud!)

Startover.

Hi, I'm Carina. So you're here, grasping this novel, open at this very page, and for that to be even possible this book must have been published!

To get this far with my novel means that I have ridden the ferocious oceans and have now arrived on the island of the unknown. My bag is pretty small, but it's quite heavy. Inside my bag, and the cause of my aching muscles, are the words 'I AM'. At first it might seem a little silly that these words are so weighted. However, once you begin thinking about it, it isn't, because they are the words that begin to define you.

I am alone in I AM. I am afraid to be alone. My name stands on its own at the beginning of this piece of writing – and if you know what it means to be Carina, then you know why it defines me. Being Carina means that I am timid, insecure, boring, irritable… fearful of sharing my work with everyone. I AM means (for me) that it's difficult to find what's great about me. So I need to work hard to find reasons to be happy with myself, but one thing I'm certain about is that I am an 'author'.

I am me because of the journey, not because of where the story ends.

Do you know what comes next? This is my journey. This is my story. Here I go… ▶

Shakela Begum says:

Hi, I'm Shakela, a creative writing and English lit student, blogger (chocolatedigestivebiscuits. wordpress.com), aspiring teacher and writer. My work is about being experimental and bringing something different to life on a page. The idea for my written piece in this anthology combines an experiment with form and my desire to become a successful writer. ▓

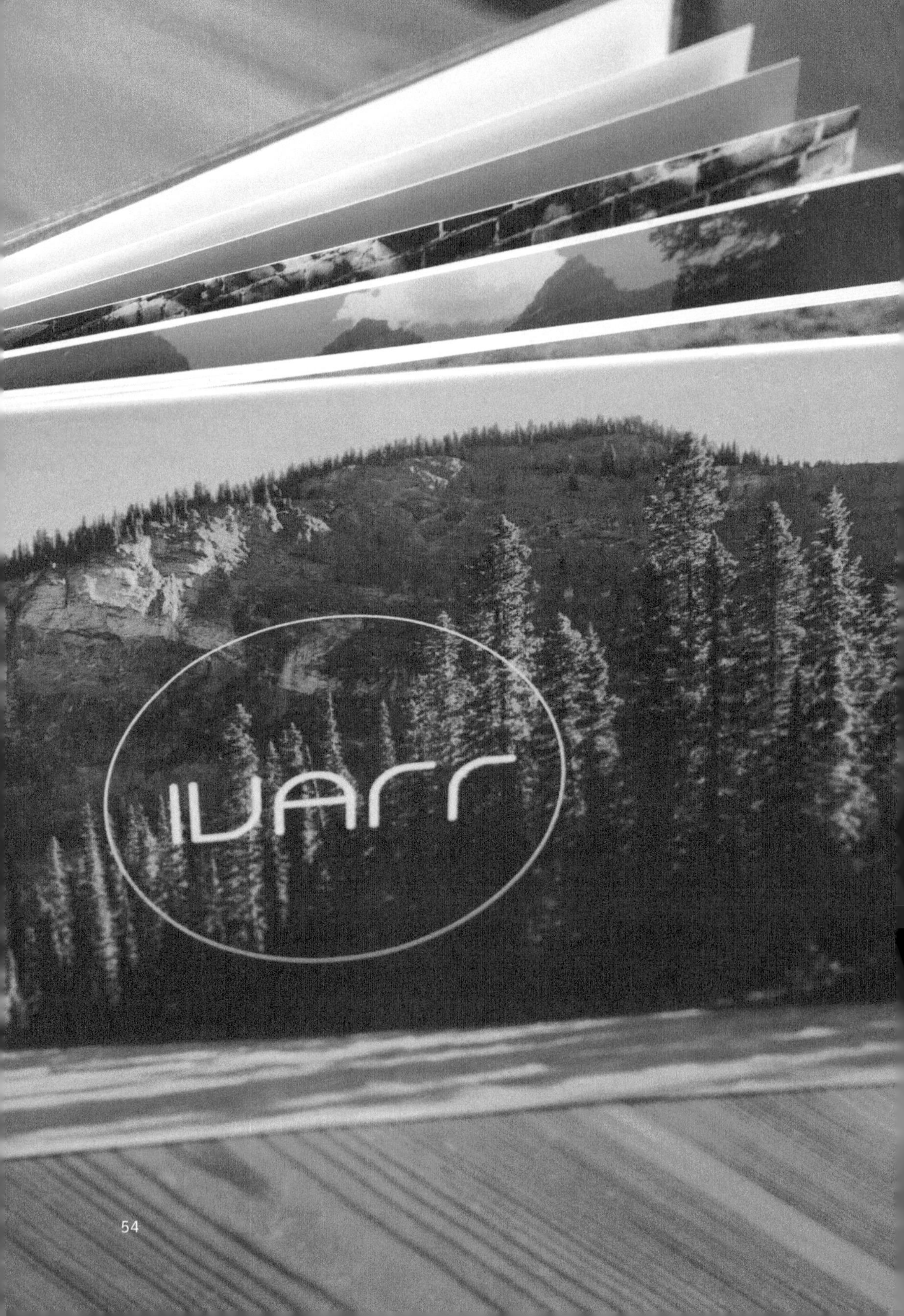

DANIEL BOYINGTON, THIRD-YEAR STUDENT,
GRAPHIC DESIGN

Shooting for perfection

Like many students, Daniel knows that freelancing is a good way into the world of work and he has already completed a number of projects for the university, including filming events and making a promotional video which involved sending up a drone camera (with permission from the police, of course).

Although self-employment is good while he's still studying, Daniel can see that it's stressful and ideally he'd like to work for a company, doing shoots for clients like Mercedes. He imagines working on an image to sell a new car. He realises there would be a tension between meeting the client brief and the design image that's in his head, but although he realises the next step up could be scary, he's excited about the potential to do what he loves and get paid for it.

One of the pieces of coursework Daniel is particularly proud of is the 'brand book'. It helped him develop some guidelines for branding himself and to think about his own future. He wants to continue developing his own approach to narrative and he'd like to go travelling, to use this experience to produce more personal work that conveys a sense of freedom and adventure.

Daniel is passionate about finding the perfect shot or the 'picture moment', as his friends call it. He thinks cinematically and will often stop in the street when he spots something he knows he could make look amazing. He believes it's his understanding of technology that gives him the ability to get the shot no one else can. ■

SAMIA DJILLI, FIRST-YEAR STUDENT,
ENGLISH LITERATURE AND CREATIVE WRITING

12 o'clock

I sit at my desk, palms sweating. It's 12 o'clock. As the rest of the office races towards the screaming kettle my hands start to shake. For everyone else 12 o'clock means a tea break. For me it means emails. On an average day emails simply mean an overwhelming amount of orders to process, but not today. Yes, the orders will still be there, but hidden among them I hope there is a particular email I have been waiting six years for.

At 22 I graduated with a first in English literature and from the moment I threw my graduation cap to the sky I gave myself a target – that I would publish a novel by the time I was 25. Of course, it was an ambitious goal and publishers are not as easy to please as I had once naively believed, but I did everything I thought would take me in the right direction.

I joined every society going, worked endless unpaid internships, kept an up-to-date blog and wrote for everyone and anyone that would allow me to. Yet at 28, with a pile of rejection letters sitting on my bedside table, my fight is yet to be won.

I sent my novel to a small publisher in south London. They called to say that they would email me by midday on 7 January if they were interested. All week I have been wracked with anxiety, but today is the day and I am hopeful.

I check my email. I have 18 messages. The first 10 are orders. My heart racing, I move to the next one. It's from Stonebox Publishers. My heart stops. "Dear Ms Milan, we are pleased to tell you we are interested in publishing your novel, but would like to work with you further on it with our editorial team..."

I look around. Everything is still, except it feels as though the whole office has been shaken upside down. Have I just been offered my dream job? ▶

Samia Djilli says:

I am 22 years old and I'm from south London. I am currently studying creative writing and English literature at the University of Greenwich in the hope of one day becoming a professional writer. My story was inspired by my own aspirations and the fear of not achieving my goals. I aim to be a published novelist, as well as working for stage and screen, and my story evolved from the idea that achieving your professional goals is not a simple task, but is ultimately worth the work. ■

JORDANA NICODEMOU, THIRD-YEAR STUDENT,
GRAPHICS

Distinctly different

"People are afraid of what's different, but different is good. None of us are the same, are we?" asks Jordana. She loves bright colours, as demonstrated by her fluorescent pink nails, and her designs have a similar vibrancy. They grab your attention – and in a busy, competitive world you have to stand out.

Jordana was bullied when she was young and it taught her how to deal with challenging relationships, to be helpful and patient, while getting your needs across. As she's got older, she's become more and more self-reliant, and that will stand her in good stead in the world of work.

She has done some work experience in an events company, which included revamping their promotional materials and which she really enjoyed, and coming from an entrepreneurial family is a real help. Jordana is considering setting up her own company and already has links with manufacturers in China. She really likes the fast pace and pressure of marketing and advertising.

A good communicator, Jordana works hard to make sure she understands what other people are trying to say and that she herself is being clear. "I'm never afraid to ask if I've understood things correctly and I'm open to feedback – it's how I learn."

Jordana can't wait to get out into the world and experience different countries and cultures. "It's exciting to think that at some point what I do will mean something for others," she muses. ∎

PURNA LOKSOM, MSC STUDENT,
ECONOMICS

Waiting for the scales of justice to tilt

Puja was the sixth child of parents from a very poor background. Her father worked in the fields of the local village. He was almost a slave and because they were of a so-called 'lower caste' their lives were very restricted. No one in Puja's family had ever had an education. It took courage, but one day Puja asked her parents to allow her to go to school. Although it wasn't easy for them to say yes, her parents agreed and, despite all the obstacles, Puja started her schooling at the age of 13.

The school was almost two hours' walk away, over hills, through jungle and across rivers. Puja spent four hours every day walking, but she studied hard and became the best student in the school. Due to her outstanding achievement, she won a scholarship, which released her family from a huge financial burden.

One monsoon evening she was walking home from school alone. In the middle of the jungle she noticed that three men were following her. Puja tried to speed up, but they came closer and closer. She was comforted when she saw her teacher was among the three men, but shocked when he led the bullying and physical harassment. She fought them, but was cruelly raped by all three and thrown into the river.

Three months later, Puja opened her eyes and found herself in bed in a mental hospital in the capital city. Surprisingly, she lost the court case, but after huge public protest and demonstration, the government forwarded the issue to the appeal court and everyone is now waiting for justice of Puja. ▶

Purna Loksom says:

I am currently doing an MSc in economics at Greenwich University as well as running my own tourism business. I enjoy research, especially into poverty reduction and equality issues, and in September 2015 I am going to do a PhD. ■

ALICE BAILEY, FOURTH-YEAR STUDENT,
BUSINESS INFORMATION SYSTEMS

Options open

Alice's mother is an inspiration to her. She describes her mum as a hard worker, someone who worked her way up in a technical role, who became a manager, who handles her significant work responsibilities professionally and earns a good salary. Alice knows she's been lucky in this respect. It's not exactly that she wants to follow in her mum's footsteps, but it's good to have such a strong role model in a busy world which sometimes offers too many options.

At the moment, Alice divides her time between lectures, revision, completing applications for graduate jobs, going to interviews, her part-time job at a museum in Greenwich and occasionally squeezing in seeing friends.

She had a great year out working in a large IT company, where she enjoyed having the opportunity to apply her skills and knowledge, and also to learn how to deal with workplace dynamics – the aspects of working life that are often described as 'soft skills', but are usually anything but... She is clear that this experience of a corporate environment is invaluable.

In terms of what Alice wants to do in future, she is slightly torn between technology and commerce. She's interested in requirements analysis, but also the life cycles of projects, services and businesses. It's easy to see hear her enthusiasm when she describes supporting a business from its early stages, taking it from something to nothing. It would also be exciting to work on a global scale, she says, and speculates about working with a company like Apple, developing products and services for different countries. ■

ORANGES ARE NOT
THE ONLY FRUIT

JEANETTE WINTERSON

'MANY CONSIDER HER TO BE THE BEST LIVING
WRITER IN THIS LANGUAGE .. . . IN HER
HANDS, WORDS ARE FLUID, RADIANT, HUMMING'

EVENING STANDARD

VINTAGE

ANA COQUET, THIRD-YEAR STUDENT,
GRAPHIC AND DIGITAL DESIGN

Accentuate the positive

Ana is one of those individuals who is pivotal in the success of any team. Someone who will think ahead, plan and remain organised; an individual who would work right up until the deadline to perfect her work and, ultimately, who is confident about making decisions. "Doubting yourself doesn't get you anywhere," she says.

At a time when university got tough and there was a significant amount of pressure just to quit, Ana did not surrender and she is proud she stuck at it.

Along with her family, Ana emigrated from Argentina in 2004, quickly settling in Peterborough. Although the transition was hard, it gave her a great new perspective on life. "I appreciate every opportunity I get. My friends and family in Argentina, or people studying in plenty of other countries, don't have anything like this. I've got a part-time job, a course I love, food and shelter. What else could I possibly ask for?"

Ana's design style has been described as rustic and homely with dashes of modernism. She loves patterns and simplicity, as well as keeping things clean and uncomplicated. What really shines through is an eye for detail and a constant focus on doing things to the utmost of her ability.

Although the future is not yet set in stone, Ana hopes to go travelling before settling down and finding out what's next. She says, "I'm curious about where I'll end up and I'm willing to take a chance just to see what happens." ∎

ABAS ABOW, INTERN

The interview

Lost, wandering apathetically in a gloom, in a hapless search to find yourself, establish yourself as a professional. How to do that among thousands just like you?

But there's a faint light; rejuvenating hope, rekindling belief. Surely having graduated gives you an upper hand? But not a hand to help you out of the quicksand.

Now you find yourself in a waiting room filled with tension, with 12 other graduates, all competing for one position – like musical chairs, but there's only one chair.

You meet your interviewer. You nervously but vigorously shake his hand as you barely but forcefully manage a smile.

You find yourself at a round table, like King Arthur and his 12 knights, and then you hear the door close. This is when it all begins.

You walk out of the room, exhale deeply and let out a huge sigh of relief. But this is not the end. No! It's just the beginning. This is when the seeds of torture, self-doubt and regret are planted, and start to slowly manifest and grow.

An enactment of the interview lingers on your mind, repeating itself over and over like a broken record.

On your journey home you acknowledge that this is your dream job, but is it the beginning or the end of your dreams? You ask yourself, "Would I be stuck in retail my whole career? There's nothing wrong with that!"

But you have dreams, ambitions, goals; you want to be an expert in your field.

You are welcomed home by a warm embrace from your beloved mother.

"How did it go, Love?" she asks.

You smile gently and respond, "It went good, Mama."

Days go by. There is no news. The doubts grow stronger, but you go on as if the interview never happened.

It's morning and your mother is yelling enthusiastically, "The letter's here!"

You race to your mother, take the letter and open it up. You hold your breath. The letter reads...

"The ending of the story is yours to write. You are the author of your own life – make it a success story!" ▶

Abas Abow says:

Hello, my name is Abas Abow and I recently graduated with a BSc in estate management from the University of Greenwich. I aspire to be a successful property manager one day. I hope to make it big and 'Dream big to make it big' is my motto in life. I know the road to success is daunting and full of obstacles, but I believe that my desire to succeed and my determination will help me avoid failure. I place my full and complete trust in God, All Mighty, and work hard for my success.

The constant struggles of job hunting and the competitive nature of finding the ideal graduate job is what inspired my story. I wanted to give a snapshot of an experience many graduates may have gone through and the turbulent feelings and emotions that they may have faced. I left a cliffhanger at the end of my story to communicate to the reader that the outcomes in their lives are all within their control if they work hard to achieve their dreams. ■

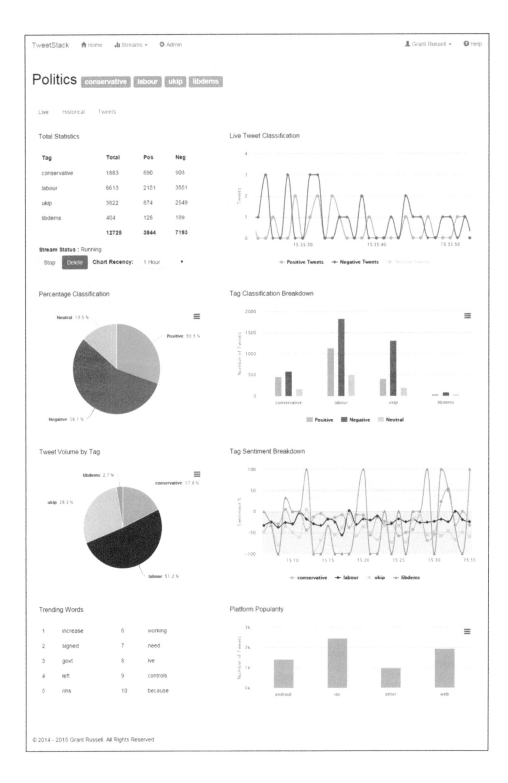

GRANT RUSSELL, FOURTH-YEAR STUDENT,
SOFTWARE ENGINEERING

Thinking big

"Our generation is going to create the technology that will exceed human capacity." Grant is clear we need to be thinking about this now as it's going to raise difficult questions for society. He recognises that the answers might be in the realms of politics, not software engineering, but what's important to him is that what he does, and the collective decisions we make, add value to society.

Grant imagines himself working for a large technology company in a development team where he has the chance to change the industry. He's excited by the prospect of helping to make life simpler and gives a great example of what he means: "What if we could use big data to discover new pieces of information that would help people and governments make smarter decisions about sustainable energy use, smart meters, that kind of thing? That would push the walls, test the limits of software engineering."

He has a huge appetite for knowledge. Any kind of feedback is good and he enjoys writing, using creative ideas and applying them in different ways, turning them into something practical in the real world. "You can build anything – the only limit is your knowledge," he says. This isn't a recent realisation. As a kid Grant built a K'nex cable car to carry his hamster across the garden, and he was coding from an early age, building websites and experimenting with what was possible.

One project he's proud of is a web application that takes live Twitter data and classifies it by sentiment (see screenshot). During the run-up to the general election he explored how it could be used in the real world by tracking data and running tests on voting experiences.

Grant is optimistic about the future. He's already applying for jobs and has got a couple of interviews. He says "The university has really delivered for me." His work placement at IBM, where he guided a team on a disaster recovery programme, has been his best experience so far. "I hope I can find a place where I can apply my interests. That's the difference – applying the knowledge," he concludes. ■

DANIELA LESKOVAR, MA STUDENT, ENGLISH: LITERARY LONDON

Cooking is love

There's something fascinating about watching food being cooked. It's the mixture of smells and sounds – pots and plates being pushed around, vegetables being chopped, eggs being cracked, and the bubbling, the sizzling and the gurgling.

The freshly cut garlic sizzled on the fire, just turning gold. It was a lovely smell. Maybe my favourite smell. Not sweet and not salty, just that state in between. It made me feel warm inside, perhaps because it reminded me of my mother cooking, smiling gently as I watched her curiously from under the table, my hands sticky with saliva and snot back then.

Throwing in the cut vegetables, the pan burned with fire. A pinch of salt, oregano, basilica, pepper –the taste must be strong – and some wine.

Mixing, mixing, mixing and up you go in the air. Heh, just a few years ago I was terrified to do that. Always thought the food would stick to the ceiling. Or the floor. Mum would make fun of me, but see me now, dear mother – I'm throwing the whole pan around and it all stays in!

Now strain the pasta, mix with the vegetables, stew them a little and onto the plate. Some cheese, parsley and a basilica leaf on top.

Cooking is love.

"Table 5 ready!" I yelled, placing the plate on the counter, where other plates waited. For a moment I admired the wild colours and the wonderful smell of meat and spices swimming around the kitchen.

The place was one big, screaming circus of rushing cooks and waiters. The chef stood in the middle of this mess, red in the face, shouting orders, and holding a sense of organization in the chaos. He was an old, round man whose hands and face told the story of the long years he'd spent in the kitchen. His strict eyes caught mine and I felt a shiver run down my spine as he rounded at me.

"Little girl, don't daydream again! Tables 7, 13, 18 and 25 are yours! Chop, chop!"

"Yes, sir!" I playfully saluted him and turned back to the stove.

Man, I do love the kitchen…

Thanks Mum. For teaching me. ■

To see what Daniela Leskovar says go to page 2.

GEORGE HARVEY, THIRD-YEAR STUDENT,
CREATIVE WRITING

Believing is achieving

James trembled. He couldn't believe what he was seeing. There, across two neat pages, were the very words he'd written about his life and disability. How could they have ended up in such a professional-looking magazine?

When he'd first written them he hadn't expected anybody to like his words. He dreamed of becoming a writer, but thought it was impossible, given his disability. Even though he studied hard and wrote daily, he was sure he'd never be as good as his favourite author, Mrs W.

James had planned on printing these words out and storing them somewhere nobody would ever see. But then his mother had noticed a printed copy he'd left on the side table. She'd hugged and praised James for how good it was, but James hadn't thought much of it. He was sure she'd only said this because he was her son, but she'd probably sent his work off to the magazine knowing he'd be too nervous to do it himself.

James heard other people reading the article, talking about how splendid and motivating it was. One lady even said she'd use it as an inspiration for her own child, who had similar problems. A warm feeling rose inside James. His writing had made a difference in someone else's life, just like Mrs W's. His efforts did pay off when he tried. And if this was what could be achieved through his mother, what could he achieve on his own?

James wrote an email to Mrs W, telling her about himself and his dreams. He knew she received lots of fan mail and probably wouldn't reply to his lengthy message, but two days later he was amazed to find Mrs W in his inbox. She gave James such wonderful advice that he printed her email and treasured it like gold. He knew the road to becoming an author would be hard and bumpy, but Mrs W had been a student once herself. If she could do it, why not him? ■

To see what George Harvey says go to page 9.

About Shared Press

SHARED PRESS
Shared Press is an independent publisher with a remit to share stories that engage with the sharp edges and messy boundaries of modern life; to give voice to new writers who care about ideas and innovation; and to inspire new creative conversations with readers.

More from Shared Press
It's a small list, but it's perfectly formed and it's growing.

Hard Change
Published by Shared Press in 2012, Dawn Reeves' *Hard Change* is set in and around the local council of a medium-sized Midlands city and centres on the compelling ramifications of the murder of a young girl. Neither a traditional political thriller nor a conventional crime novel, it focuses on strategy rather than procedure and examines whether – and how – individual and collective action can make a difference.

Change the Ending
What can fiction offer the public sector? A new perspective? An alternative way of working? Inspiration for the future? In *Change the Ending*, an intriguing collection of 350-word stories, senior local government officers, accountants, people in public health, social workers and many others rise to the challenge. The results are amazing – imaginative, forward-thinking, often celebratory, always stimulating. These are stories that matter.

About Dawn Reeves

Dawn is a successful facilitator, trainer and writer. A former director in a large public sector organisation, she now works with a range of clients looking for creative approaches to making change happen. Her energy and enthusiasm for this work come from a deep curiosity about the world and a drive to collaborate with the people she works with.

For *Making Our Mark*, she ran creative thinking and writing workshops for Greenwich University students, collaborated on creative conversations, and curated the publication that resulted from the project.

Dawn lives in London and travels widely.

Contact her via **dawn@dawnreeves.com**

For updates on new projects and titles, see **sharedpress.co.uk**

Lightning Source UK Ltd.
Milton Keynes UK
UKOW07f1411130515

251455UK00001B/1/P

9 780957 498150